Acting Edition

Sandra

Written by David Cale

Music by
Matthew Dean Marsh

No one shall make any changes in this title(s) for the purpose of production. No part of this book may be reproduced, stored in a retrieval system, scanned, uploaded, or transmitted in any form, by any means, now known or yet to be invented, including mechanical, electronic, digital, photocopying, recording, videotaping, or otherwise, without the prior written permission of the publisher. No one shall share this title(s), or any part of this title(s), through any social media or file hosting websites.

For all inquiries regarding motion picture, television, online/digital and other media rights, please contact Concord Theatricals Corp.

MUSIC AND THIRD-PARTY MATERIALS USE NOTE

Licensees are solely responsible for obtaining formal written permission from copyright owners to use copyrighted music and/or other copyrighted third-party materials (e.g. artworks, logos) in the performance of this play and are strongly cautioned to do so. If no such permission is obtained by the licensee, then the licensee must use only original music and materials that the licensee owns and controls. Licensees are solely responsible and liable for clearances of all third-party copyrighted materials, including without limitation music, and shall indemnify the copyright owners of the play(s) and their licensing agent, Concord Theatricals Corp., against any costs, expenses, losses and liabilities arising from the use of such copyrighted third-party materials by licensees. For music, please contact the appropriate music licensing authority in your territory for the rights to any incidental music.

IMPORTANT BILLING AND CREDIT REQUIREMENTS

If you have obtained performance rights to this title, please refer to your licensing agreement for important billing and credit requirements.

SANDRA was first produced in New York City by the Vineyard Theatre (Douglas Aibel, Artistic Director; Sarah Stern, Artistic Director; Suzanne Appel, Managing Director) and premiered on November 3, 2022. The director was Leigh Silverman, and the music was by Matthew Dean Marsh. The artistic team for the production included scenic design by Rachel Hauck, costume design by Linda Cho, lighting design by Thom Weaver and sound design by Kathy Ruvuna. The production stage manager was Katie Ailinger. The cast was as follows:

SANDRA JONES/SANDRA RIVERS . . . . Marjan Neshat

CHARACTERS

SANDRA JONES/SANDRA RIVERS

SETTING

Crown Heights, Brooklyn, New York;
Puerto Vallarta and Cozumel, Mexico;
and Jenner, Northern California.

AUTHOR'S NOTES

Regarding the age range of the actor portraying Sandra. I imagined Sandra as being in her mid-forties, but I would say between forty and fifty-five years, any younger detracts from the heart of the story, and is at odds with where Sandra is at in her life. If it feels resonant with an actor over fifty-five, then that works for me too.

I intended for Sandra to be able to be portrayed by an actor of any race or heritage. On page 46, where Sandra speaks of her mother's maiden name, the production has the liberty to tweak the name, so it's appropriate for the heritage of the actor who's portraying Sandra, i.e. if Sandra is played by a Korean-American actor, a Korean last name may be substituted, if an Iranian-American actor, similarly, etc, etc. If there's no need to adjust the name, leave as it is in the script.

Productions must use the recordings of the play's solo piano music performed by Matthew Dean Marsh. They are essentially a character in the show.

At the end of the script is a detailed list of cue timings.

To Matthew

I'd made dinner for Ethan.

I'd wanted us to have a quiet evening together before he went off on his trip to Mexico. A few days earlier he'd performed some of his piano compositions at a club on the Lower East Side. It was a spellbinding performance.

He came into my apartment holding a small envelope.

Said, "It's my CD that I never released. It has all the piano pieces I played the other night. You're the only person I'm giving it to. And I did a little drawing on the cover, of you wading in the sea."

I was very touched, thanked him, said, "I'm going to put it on now. I'm so glad I hung on to the CD player!"

He said, "Listen to it later. I just hear all the mistakes."

And we sat down to eat.

I was encouraging him to book more gigs. To keep the momentum going. He said maybe show business wasn't for him. Maybe he should be a cook. I said that was ridiculous. He's so gifted. He just needed to persevere.

He asked how things were at my café. I told him a woman had come in today and just sat down on the floor and wouldn't move, because she said she was upset that we'd discontinued the blueberry scones. I told her we'd never actually had blueberry scones, and she said she must have gotten the wrong café and got up off the floor and left. That that was my most eventful occurrence of the day.

He said the scone lady story made him want something sweet. We had dessert, and he had to leave to go pack, as it was an early flight.

At the door, I hugged him goodbye and he said, "I feel like disappearing from my life. Part of me just isn't in the world. I'm at a remove."

I said, "Even from me?"

"No, not you," he said, "But you and I are so simpatico, if I vanish you'd probably disappear from your life too. I love you, Sandra. I love you so much."

I said, "I love you too, Ethan. Have fun in Mexico."

We hugged again and he left.

Two and a half weeks later I thought, it's odd Ethan hasn't been in touch. He must be back. And just as I was thinking this, I received a phone message –

"Hi, my name is Laurie. Your name and number are listed as Ethan Martin's 'in case of an emergency' person to call. Do you know where he is? We don't know if we should call the police."

For the next days I walked around feeling as though a small bomb had gone off inside me.

Two detectives came by the café to interview me. One was friendly and sympathetic. The other was officious. He did most of the questioning. He asked if I had any theories of where Ethan might be? What state of mind he was in? He asked if we were romantically involved. I answered, "No, Ethan is gay." And that was when I felt the tone of the questions shifted.

"Is Ethan promiscuous?"

"I wouldn't call him promiscuous. He likes boys."

"Is he prone to picking up strangers?"

"Occasionally."

"Drugs? Crystal meth? Cocaine?"

"He's sober."

"You sure about that?"

"Yes, I'm sure."

"So he has done drugs?"

"In the past."

"What would happen when he did them?"

"He would get into situations that weren't good for him."

"What kind of situations?"

"Sexual situations."

The friendlier one stepped in and said, "We know Ethan never boarded the plane back from Puerto Vallarta."

He asked if I had contact information for his family. I told him that Ethan came out to his parents when he was fifteen, and they threw him out of the house. That he hadn't had anything to do with them since.

He asked, "What did a homeless fifteen-year-old gay kid do to survive?"

I said, "I think he did whatever he felt he needed to do. He hasn't had an easy life."

He asked if I had a recent photo. I texted him a good one I'd taken of Ethan last year, on his thirty-first birthday.

A week or so later still no further clues had come to light.

I felt so generally shaken I bought a bottle of wine, and downed the whole bottle in one evening.

I woke up hung over, thinking, when I'm alone I can't just have one drink. I know this. I can't be trusted to have wine in the house. Then I remembered what I'd done last night.

Oh Lord, I thought as I checked my emails. There it was: Email Confirmation – Supersaver Special – one non-refundable return flight to Puerto Vallarta and hotel accommodation plus complimentary breakfast, leaving for Mexico on Monday morning.

Name of Passenger: Sandra Jones.

I thought, what am I gonna do? This is absurd. I can't believe I did this. Well, you've paid for it now. You may as well go. The café will be fine. Maybe you will find Ethan. And three days later I'm boarding a plane for Mexico.

> *The lights shift and we hear the subtle sounds of a plane.*
>
> *Sandra looks to her left for a moment and the lighting suggests light coming in through a plane window.*
>
> *The sounds of the plane fade along with the lights.*

The first day in Puerto Vallarta my thoughts run the gamut from worrying Ethan has had a drug relapse, he's been kidnapped, gay bashed, is injured somewhere, oh Lord, the thought of someone hurting him; to thinking, maybe he'd planned this. And becoming furious with him. To stopping on the street and thinking, what the hell am I doing here?

I'm at an outdoor café, having lunch, writing in my journal.

I look up and coming towards me I see a dapperly dressed, quite flamboyant-seeming man probably in his seventies accompanied by a bearded guy. Around thirty. With very long scraggly blondish-brown hair that went halfway down his back.

The two of them sit at the empty table next to mine.

I'm writing in my journal, so I'm not paying much attention.

I hear the older man speak. He has that vaguely Southern accent some gay men seem to naturally acquire even though they've never been anywhere near the south.

"I'm going to be very direct. I think you are gorgeous," he says to this long-haired guy. "Well, I better take my insulin."

And he gets up clutching a small purse-like bag. Heads to the restroom.

The second he's out of view the younger guy swiftly gets up from the table. Briskly walks across the square, his long mane of hair catching the breeze.

The man comes back from the restroom, "Where'd he go?"

"I think he left."

"Did it look like he was coming back?"

"No, it looked like he felt a sense of urgency about leaving."

"Guess I must have been too forthcoming regarding the way I felt. Well, I'll be."

> *He gazes in the direction his table companion has gone, then focuses on Sandra.*

"You're American? My name's Beauford. My mother was an artist. She named me after the painter, Beauford Delaney. Well, I'll be."

Beauford again looks back out in the direction of his former table companion.

He sits back down appearing a little shaken.

I say to him, "I hope I'm not being too intrusive, but if you don't mind me asking, who was he?"

"You know, I'm seventy years old. Someone tells me their name it goes in one ear out the other. He told me his name when we met and I said to him on the way here, 'I've forgotten your name, please tell me again.' He told me and it plum straight slipped away. In my defense it was a name I was not that familiar with. What's your name?"

"Sandra."

"Sandra," he says, "Sandra. Like Sandra Cisneros, the poet. I'll remember that. Sandra."

"So you just met?"

"Yes, he came up to me on the beach, started conversing. I thought he was trying to pick me up. We had an interesting conversation. He told me he liked to write his innermost thoughts on pieces of paper and put them into bottles, seal the bottles and toss them into the sea. He asked if I want to come with him to get some paper and bottles and try it. I told him I was diabetic and needed to get to get an orange juice, give myself a shot. He brought me to this café and now... I'm going to order a fruit juice for my blood sugar and a cocktail for my nerves. Can I procure you a beverage?"

I thought about the promise I'd made to myself not to have alcohol. Then I said, "That's very kind. You know what, Yes, I'd love a cocktail."

"Try the Charo Negro, they're very good in this town. Scoot over if you like."

We order drinks. He asks me how long I'm staying in Puerto Vallarta?

"Just a week."

"It's a lovely place to vacation."

"I'm not really vacationing. My closest friend Ethan came to Puerto Vallarta four weeks ago and he never came back. No-one's heard anything from him. He checked out of the room he was staying in and disappeared. He had told me he wanted to use Puerto Vallarta as a base and he might take some excursions. We don't know if he did. The only thing that's known, according to the authorities, is he didn't leave Mexico."

"So you've come here looking for a missing loved one? Oh, I am so sorry."

"Are you on vacation?"

"My aunt left me a small inheritance and I'm wandering around the gay friendly resorts of the world. Looking for a lovely love affair. But I guess these things are like rare and elusive birds who never show up if you set out to look for them."

Beauford lives on Riverside Drive. He doesn't have a cell phone or email address, so I write down his home number, give him my cell number and we go our separate ways.

Next few days I wander around Puerto Vallarta looking for someone, who in my bones, I sense isn't there.

On the flight home I remember that I have a couple of Mexican newspapers in my bag. My Spanish isn't great, but it'll at least give me something to look at.

Then I see it.

The headline –

"Mensajes en una botella"

Messages in a bottle.

Kids have been finding bottles washed up on the beach with hand-written notes inside them. Written in English.

Accompanying the story is a photo of a boy holding up one of the bottles with the note inside it.

And a second photo of one of the notes.

It's written with immaculate penmanship.

It reads –

"I want to kiss you so badly"

Oh my God, that's Ethan's handwriting. I'm certain of it. And that's the kind of thing Ethan would say. That long-haired guy with Beauford must have met Ethan.

I guess I appear suddenly stricken because the flight attendant asks me if I'm okay?

"Yes," I say, "Thank you. Can you bring me a white wine?"

 Lights shift.

Special agent Stephen McCourt, comes to the café with a photographer. From the time I opened the place Ethan, because he had such beautiful handwriting, would write up the menu on the chalkboard.

The photographer takes photos of the board, leaves me with Stephen as I try to describe a man I'd barely looked at. But there can't be many Caucasian men in Puerto Vallarta with hair halfway down their back.

I call Beauford to see if anything else comes to mind for him about this guy. His outgoing phone message is, "If you're hearing this I'm still wandering the world and will call you upon my return."

Two more weeks go by and beyond a handwriting expert confirming it was Ethan's writing on the note in the bottle, it feels like the energy is going out of the search to find him. I want to shame Stephen into increased action, I say, "Nothing seems to be happening, I'm going to go back to Puerto Vallarta. I'm going to look for this long-haired guy myself."

Stephen says, "That's obviously not a good idea."

I thought I was bluffing, but as soon as the words come out of me, it instinctively makes a kind of sense.

Sara, the café manager, wants me to take some time off, for "self-care."

"You have serious marriage issues to work out. Now your closest friend has disappeared. It's a lot. And what if you find this person? You may be putting yourself in danger."

"Something is telling me to go back to Mexico. I can't explain it. Something is telling me to go."

> *We hear very discreet street sounds and mariachi music.*

> *Sandra stands.*

> *The visual look of the stage changes.*

It's a strange feeling to walk around a town you don't really know, looking for a man you've never met. And all you have to go on is he has exceptionally long hair and a beard.

I walk on the beach looking.

I go into restaurants. Scan them. Walk out.

Bars.

Clubs.

I literally see no men with hair longer than their shoulder.

On day three I take myself in hand.

What are you doing?

Stop this. It's crazy and futile.

Go lay on the beach.

Let the police and the FBI do their job.

The discreet street sounds drift away.

I'm walking on the sand, looking for a place to sit, when I hear, "Sandra! Sandra!"

She turns to look in the direction of her name being called.

Two regulars from my café – Maggie and Peter Raymond – are laying on a large beach blanket with a couple of friends. Seeing their faces is a relief. They ask if I'm with my husband. I tell them, "No, we're separated at the moment, I'm here on my own," and we make a plan to get a drink later at Bar Paloma.

I'm sitting at the bar when Peter and Maggie come in with three people. The other couple from the beach and a palpably sexy man.

The place is crowded, but there're five empty seats up the bar, which they take. I glance at this gorgeous guy and all I can think is, damn, have mercy.

I'm so spellbound by him that I accidentally knock over my cocktail. He leaps into action to mop it up with a napkin.

"I guess that's a sign I shouldn't be drinking," I say.

We order drinks.

I tell them the reason I'm in Puerto Vallarta.

Peter says, "I think more people go missing than you would imagine. And the fact Ethan checked out of the hotel. It does seem as though he deliberately went somewhere. Speaking of which, we're going off on an evening trip to Islas Marietas. Good luck. We will of course see you back at 'Sandra's.'"

The four leave and the gorgeous man stays, and finally speaks.

He has an Italian accent. Mixed with something else. A potpourri of a voice.

He asks, "What are you going to do when you find him? This guy you're looking for."

"I'm going to find out what he knows."

"What if he's a dangerous person?"

"I'm a New Yorker. I don't frighten easily."

"Oh, oh, oh, you're a tough girl, are you? Yeah?"

"No. But I don't think they're doing enough to find him. I can't help feeling it's because Ethan's gay. I think if he was a straight jock they'd be all over it."

"I'm going to have another, can I buy you a drink? So, tell me, what is 'Sandra's'?"

"It's my café in Crown Heights. Brooklyn. We were never actually introduced. I'm Sandra. Sandra Jones."

"I'm Luca," he says, "Luca Messina."

"Your accent. Where are you from?"

"My father's Italian. My mother was Irish. I was born in America and raised half my childhood in New York City and the other half in Sicily. Right now I live in Mexico. And I'm going to school at Universad Anáhuac. I know, I'm a bit old to still be going to school. I'm thirty-three, but I'm not the oldest one in my classes."

"Where's Universad Anáhuac?"

"It's in Mexico City."

He looks at me with these seductive brown eyes and after a long loaded up pause says, "I hope you find your friend," leans over and hugs me, which seems awfully physically forward.

His cheek is alongside my cheek for a long moment.

I think, I've never held in my arms a man I felt so physically attracted to.

He sits back down. Points to my wedding ring.

"You're married?"

"Separated. For the last two months. We've been talking about getting back together. Richard, my husband, wants to. But I think it's over."

Why am I not telling the truth? I was the one who was trying to get back together with Richard.

"How long were you married?"

"Thirteen years. But it's come to an end."

I don't really think it's come to an end. But I'm so attracted to this man I don't want to have anything get in the way of the course it feels like it's on.

"Are you hungry? I know a good place."

I'm not hungry, but this man is so compelling, I go along.

We go to a tiny, hole-in-the-wall restaurant.

As we walk our bodies lightly brush.

It almost feels deliberate on his part.

We eat.

Luca tells me he's studying Mexican and English literature. He speaks four languages. He's a student, but he's also a playwright. He swims every day. And he's so captivating.

After the meal he shows me around town.

We stop and listen to some musicians playing on the street, and he walks me back to my hotel.

Asks if there's a toilet in the lobby. The bathrooms are under repair.

I say, "Just come up. Use mine."

When we get in my room I have a sudden panic. I've let a complete stranger come up to my room! What am I doing? I don't know this man. This is unsafe. Maybe he's some kind of gigolo. I think, well he's friends with Maggie and Peter Raymond, so he's not totally off the street.

All this as he's peeing with the bathroom door open, which strikes me as odd, but then I think, maybe it's an Italian thing, I don't know.

He washes his hands, comes out and puts his arms around me.

"Oh, Sandra," he says, "I like you."

Our cheeks are brushing. He's moving his head. I'm thinking, are we gonna kiss? Are we gonna kiss?

We kiss.

He has the softest, most sensuous lips.

For a moment I have a fear that maybe I've forgotten how to kiss. My husband and I haven't been physical with each other for so long. It all quickly comes back to me. He pulls himself away.

"I'm weak. I can't control myself with you. You're married. I should go."

I say, "It doesn't matter. Come on."

I think, I need to do this. I need to be physically intimate with someone.

We go to the bedroom.

He says, "I'm sweaty."

"I don't care."

He takes off his clothes.

I've been with the same man for thirteen years of marriage and seven years before that. Luca's physically so different to Richard. He's taller. He's broader. His body is almost completely smooth. On his upper left arm, he has a single tattoo. He's a swimmer and his body reflects it.

"What about your husband?"

"It's over. I'm separated. It's past."

He helps me out of my clothes.

We're on the bed.

He's on top of me.

I need to be sexual with someone who is not my husband. I need to feel someone attracted to me. I need to do this, I think.

He has a wide grin as he pushes himself slightly inside me and then back out.

He asks, "Does it feel nice?"

I say, "It feels incredible."

"Yes?"

"Yes. Incredible.

Yes.

Yes.

Yes."

And in my head I'm thinking, my marriage really is over.

The lights slowly dim to an intimately low level where we can barely see Sandra.

SOUND CUE NO. 1: *In the near dark we hear a recording of an original piano composition from Ethan's CD entitled –*

"LOVE THEME FROM AN IMAGINARY MOVIE ENTITLED SANDRA"

We are with Sandra and Luca, at night, post physical intimacy.

They are in bed.

There is a considerable pause in the speech as the music continues to establish itself.

The scene is hushed and spoken over the composition.

"What is this music?"

"It's my friend Ethan. He's a composer. He recorded tracks for an album, but he's never released them. I have all the recordings on my phone."

"It's nice to lay around in bed with you."

"Yes.

Pause, as the music plays.

I spoke to Ethan almost every day. It's like half my life has vanished. But we're very psychic with one another. He'll cross my mind and a second later he'll text me. Or if I'm feeling down, he'll suddenly call on the phone. I think if he were no longer alive, I'd feel it."

"I'll come with you to look for this long-haired guy. You shouldn't be doing this alone. And I feel like I've seen him on the beach. With blond in the hair?"

"Yes."

"I'll go with you."

The music plays.

"I keep thinking I'll find clues in the music he gave me. It's all solo piano. There are no lyrics. So I've been scrutinizing the track titles."

"The piece of music you just put on. Does it have a name?"

"This one? Yes."

"What is it?"

"I'm embarrassed to say."

"Tell me."

"'Love Theme from an Imaginary Movie Entitled Sandra.' That's the title."

"Yeah?"

"Yeah."

"So we're in an imaginary movie right now?"

"Yes."

"It doesn't feel imaginary to me... Come here."

The recording of "LOVE THEME FROM AN IMAGINARY MOVIE ENTITLED SANDRA" *continues playing for a few moments.*

Sandra stands, and we are out of the bedroom scene.

The music continues.

The following morning, while Luca's still sleeping I go into the bathroom, and take off my wedding ring.

She breaks down.

"This is so fucking sad. And scary."

Recovering.

Wrap it in tissues and tuck it in my purse.

The music ends.

Later that day, Luca and I walk through the streets of Puerto Vallarta looking for this man I'd sat next to in the café with Beauford.

Occasionally he'll hold my hand. I've never been with anyone so physically demonstrative. It makes me think of Richard. If I tried to hold Richard's hand on the street he'd say, "What are you doing? We're not kids." Not that I necessarily want to hold a man's hand, but I'd like the option. I tell myself, I'm not cheating on my husband. Richard was the one who wanted to separate.

We carry on walking.

I remembered how, even as a kid, watching my mother with my father, I made this big pronouncement, that I would never be in a compromised relationship. And I got this sudden sinking feeling in my stomach. That's most certainly what I'm in with Richard. I remembered Ethan once saying I was inhibited around my husband and he didn't like to see me like that.

We arrive at the beach and Luca suddenly...

"Sandra, look!"

Sandra sharply moves her arm up and points, emulating Luca's move.

A few feet from the shore there's a man with hair more than halfway down his back and a beard.

"He's much blonder. The guy I sat next to wasn't that blonde."

Luca tells me I'm being naïve. "Men dye their hair all the time."

I say I want to speak to him on my own.

Luca insists on standing nearby, in case there's any trouble.

I say, "If everything's okay, I'll wave. If I need you to come over and rescue me, I'll put my hand on my hips."

> *She demonstrates the "hand on hips" alarm pose.*

As I approach this man on the beach a wave of fear engulfs me.

What am I doing?

This is for the police.

Nonetheless, I stand on the shore about fifteen feet away from him. He catches me staring.

> *He's Australian, and Sandra adopts his accent when quoting him.*

"It's beautiful, no? Hypnotizing. I could stand here all day watching the waves."

"Yes... Have you come across any bottles with messages inside? I was reading that some have been washing up on the shore."

He says people throwing glass into the ocean sickens him. He's a surfer, he says. The sea means a lot to him. Though of late he's a reluctant model. We get into a conversation. He tells me he'd appeared in a cell phone commercial that was popular in Australia, which had him talking on a cell phone while surfing. It had made him, "a boatload of unexpected money and me and the fiancée took this trip to Mexico as a treat. She's an actress, and a Tennessee Williams nut. She'd wanted to come to Puerto Vallarta because a movie based on the

Tennessee Williams play, *The Night of the Lizard*, was filmed here."

"I think it's an Iguana. *The Night of the Iguana.*"

"Oh, you know what, you're right."

I wave at Luca, who waves back and leaves.

The Australian says, "Well, enjoy the water," and moves away slightly.

I take off my shoes, take out my phone, put on headphones...

> **SOUND CUE NO. 2:** *We hear what Sandra is hearing in her headphones, as another track from Ethan's CD begins to play.*
>
> *The track is entitled –*

"FURTHER AND FURTHER"

...and walk a little way into the sea.

> *Sandra takes a step forward going further into the sea.*

Then further.

> *And another.*

And further.

> *And another.*
>
> *The music plays as Sandra looks out across the waves.*
>
> *The sound of the sea is woven into the recording.*
>
> *She speaks as the music plays.*

I wish I could swim with the music playing in my ears.

I wish I could go far out to sea with the music in my head.

I imagine drowning with the music coursing through me.

I wonder, what will be the last thing I hear in my life?

I think, what will be the last words anyone says to me?

And who will say them?

What will be the last thing I'll see?

Who will be the last person I speak to in my life?

When I get to the end and look back, who will I have loved the most?

If I'm honest with myself, who have I loved the most?

A child swimming underwater bumps into my leg.

I hear the Australian surfer call out, "Don't drop your phone."

And myself answer, "I won't."

I take off the headphones.

> *The piano composition* "FURTHER AND FURTHER" *stops abruptly.*

Start to wade back to the shore.

This little kid calls out to a woman on the beach, "Look Mama, I'm dissolving!"

And begins to lower himself under the water, then jumps up and calls out, "Not really!"

And starts giggling like a maniac, as though it's the funniest thing he's ever done in his life.

I look up at the sky, and suddenly feel enormously happy to be alive.

The sounds of the sea fade.

The lights change dramatically, and we are out of the scene.

I'm walking back to my hotel when it hits me. I just became Ethan's drawing of me on the front of the CD.

I see Luca the following day.

He reads a poem every morning. Even if it's a bad poem, he says. "A bad poem is better than no poem. Best is to learn good poems, so they live inside you." He sits cross-legged on the bed in his underwear telling me about different poets. Says when he finishes school he'll probably be a teacher. Go back to Italy and be the poetry and literature professor in a village. Teach poor children how to read. And I have the sudden image in my head of myself trailing around an Italian village following Luca and a pack of schoolchildren responding to their teacher as if he were the Pied Piper.

I see him the next day, and the next day and the next.

He starts drinking wine and cocktails from first thing in the morning. I think again, well maybe it's cultural, but one thing's for sure, it's not helping me give up alcohol.

He begins to open up to me about his family.

She recalls what Luca has said in his voice.
He shakes his head in disapproval.

"Money just comes to my father. Money has shitty taste in men."

"What about your mother?"

He shrugs.

"My father said she ran away back to Iowa or Ireland where she was from. But I don't know. I don't know."

"My mother was gone suddenly too. Well, so was my father. I was raised mostly by my step-father. He was a musician. I grew up with bands in the living room, rehearsing into the night."

The lights change and draw us out of the little scene.

I want to take photos of Luca on my phone. But he doesn't want that.

"We're not on show for social media. It's private what we have. It takes away its power if you start wearing it in public."

It's true I mainly wanted to take pictures of us to post on Instagram and Facebook to be scandalous. To suggest to anyone who might see that I'm not the straight-laced married woman, I'm someone who's obviously having a wild affair with a gorgeous Italian guy in Mexico.

But I also wanted souvenirs to prove to myself I was attractive enough to attract a sexy looking man.

Time passing has made me so insecure.

And the feeling of some kind of sexual invisibility approaching.

I get back to Brooklyn in a daze.

I can't get Luca out of my thoughts.

I say to Sara at the café, "It's so sexy between he and I. And easy. He's the kind of person I always thought I would be with. I could really marry this guy."

Sara says, "You're already married! I thought you were trying to reconcile with your husband."

I say, "I don't think I can go back. I got a taste of something I always wanted with Luca, that I'd come to believe didn't exist for me. I'm so shaken by Ethan's disappearance; Luca pulls me out of myself. Richard is behaving unbelievably coldly right now. This man I barely know is being so kind."

"I just have to say it; I think it's weird this guy is coming on to you so strong the moment you meet."

Sara and I have known each other a lot of years. I love her, but she has a need to be the attractive one in our relationship. When anyone becomes even the slightest bit flirtatious with me in the café, in her eyes they must want something. They can't just be attracted to me. There has to be some dark ulterior motive.

I wish I hadn't told her about Luca. I make a promise to myself that from this point on, I'm not talking about him to anyone. It is private.

I get a message; Ethan's friends are having a "support gathering" in a restaurant. I don't want to go. I know I'll be the oldest person there and don't feel like feeling an age difference right now, but then it's weird if I don't show up. Anyway, I go. And of course, it turns out to be the right thing to do. All the friends are fearing the worst, that something terrible has happened. That Ethan is dead. I don't say anything, but my instincts are telling me that just isn't so.

Special Agent Stephen McCourt calls and says the missing person flyers are now up around Puerto Vallarta. He tells me Ethan's cell phone and his email haven't been used since he disappeared. He says, "I probably shouldn't be telling you this, but before he left, Ethan emptied his bank account and closed it."

"He did? So maybe he planned this? Have other young American men gone missing in Mexico?"

"Yes."

"Were they gay?"

He has no idea.

I do a google search for "Missing man Puerto Vallarta." "Missing American Mexico." I find an article in a local paper in Southern California about a David Zander who vanished in Cozumel. There's someone quoted in the article speculating he may have been abducted by a drug cartel to extort money from the Zander family, who it seems are very wealthy. That he had $30,000 in cash with him.

Someone named Cory Calhoun disappeared, also in Cozumel. At the end of the article it says, "If you have any information, please contact findingcory@gmail." I write. Ask, "Has anything come to light for them?" And a young man, Liam, calls me.

> *She mimes the phone conversation, adopting Liam's voice.*

"Cory's body washed up on the beach. The authorities said it was an accidental drowning, but there's no way Cory would go in the sea. I think he was murdered, but no-one else feels the same way, and they look at me like I'm a hysterical, crazy person when I say it. Oh, and Cory was in his underwear. Do you think your friend Ethan was murdered?"

"I don't."

Liam says, "Oh," and goes quiet on the other end of the line.

> *She hangs up.*

Luca starts calling me on FaceTime to see how I am and if there are any developments.

I say, "You're the only person that doesn't seem to think I'm in denial believing Ethan is alive."

"Your instincts tell you. You have to listen to them."

He's found a translation of Lorca poems that he approves of. He's reading me poetry over FaceTime.

He's so seductive. I can feel myself being drawn more and more into him.

He says, "You make me feel fresh. I was so bored with myself. Now you make me feel I'm okay."

I say, "That's what it is for me too. I feel fresh with you."

He says he thought our relationship would just be fun but that he's falling in love with me.

"I love you, Sandra," he says.

And I find myself telling someone "I love you" for the first time, via FaceTime. Though I can't quite tell how deeply I mean it.

Peter and Maggie, who I'd run into in Puerto Vallarta, come into the café and, after just promising myself that I won't talk about it to anyone, I make a beeline for their table and immediately blurt out, "You probably know this, but after we all met in the bar, I spent much of the rest of my time in Mexico with Luca. In fact, we're having a little bit of an affair. Well, it's more than a little bit. I think it's turning into something serious."

They look at me blankly.

Ask, "Who's Luca?"

I say, "Your friend who was with you at the bar... The very good-looking guy you were with."

Peter says, "Oh he wasn't with us. He came in the bar at the same time. We thought you knew him."

I say, "I thought he was with you."

"No," Peter says, "we'd never seen him before. None of us had."

I FaceTime call Luca.

"That day we met, I thought you were with my friends."

"Oh no, we all just walked in together."

"So we just randomly met."

"Yes, the only available seat was up at the bar with you and your friends. Fate! Fate! Fate!"

"Have you been drinking?"

"Drowning my sorries 'cause I miss you. I miss you!"

And when we hung up I think, I picked up a total stranger. I've never done that in my life. I picked up a stranger in a bar.

I say to Sara, "I'm going to go back to Mexico for a few days. I'll take the laptop with me. I can work from there."

Sara says, "Sandra, what are you doing? The finances of the café are not in good shape. And I've been putting off telling you this because of all you were going through, but my husband and I don't want to live here anymore. We're moving to Montreal in a month and a half. You have to replace me."

"I'm shocked. You've been with me from almost the beginning."

"I'm sorry it's coming up now. And I don't know what to say, I thought you wanted to work on your marriage. I can't help but feel you're hiding from your life in this whole thing with Luca."

I say, "I know it will probably end when he goes back to school, but I have to see this through."

"Don't lose a good-hearted man because you're intoxicated by a fling," she says.

"I'm not so sure these days that Richard's such a good-hearted man. I think he's selectively good-hearted, but I'm having dinner with him tonight."

A dinner which goes something like this.

I ask Richard, "What happened with us?"

He answers, "Why do we need to talk about that?"

"I think it would help us if we talked about it."

"We were two people who'd never had a relationship, who were having one for the first time. And what should probably have only lasted a month we managed to spin out to twenty years. You should be with an artistic person. I'm not exciting to you. You're like a little girl that needs a lot of stimulation."

"I'm not a little girl, Richard. I'm an adult who wants to be with someone who they feel is happy to be with them. Why do I always feel like you're attacking me?"

"Maybe you should talk to a therapist about that."

"I'm tired of trying to win you over. There's always this underlying feeling that I'm some kind of disappointment to you."

"I think it's more that you're a disappointment to yourself. Because you're stuck. You've been stuck for years and you don't have the guts to do anything about it."

"I met someone in Mexico."

"Oh, fuck off!"

He gets up from the table. Walks out the restaurant.

Three days later I come home to the apartment, and the couch is gone.

The dining table is gone.

The paintings on the walls are gone.

Richard has even piled up my clothes neatly on the floor and taken the chest of drawers they were in.

The only furniture left aside from the bed is a single chair.

I walked into the apartment and literally gasped.

Lights shift to a dramatically different look.

Walking out of the airport, it's a relief to be back in Puerto Vallarta. And for the first time, Luca invites me to the place where he lives.

The stage environment distinctly shifts lighting-wise.

It's a little cottage on the outskirts of Puerto Vallarta.

While he's at the store buying coffee I look around. See women's clothes hanging in the closet.

I think, you don't have any kind of exclusive hold on him. He's a very good looking thirty-three-year-old in great physical shape. He goes swimming every morning. Come to your senses before you start completely making a fool of yourself.

Luca sleeps about ten hours. I know I don't get enough rest. I run on three or four hours sleep some nights.

Next morning I'm up at five a.m. He's never awake at that hour.

I get out of bed. Wander around the living room. See a note pasted on the wall by a desk.

Internet

With the name – Rosaroja

and

– La contraseña

With a password-like number next to it.

I type it all into my laptop, it works.

And I get back into bed with the computer, do some housekeeping for the café.

I start re-reading the article about the missing boy David Zander. Out of curiosity I go to Facebook. Type in his name. There are hundreds of David Zanders.

I start clicking on each one. Just as I'm thinking, this is ridiculous, I come to a David Zander where the first post is "We miss you David." There are many other similar messages, people asking if there's any new information regarding his disappearance. He's a very pretty blond boy.

I look at the photos section. There are several pictures of him in Cozumel.

Then I see it – a photo of David Zander standing on the beach with a guy with long hair halfway down his back and a beard. He's wearing a tank top. It has to be the long-haired guy with Beauford. But you can't really see his face.

I take a screenshot of the photo. Enlarge it. Scrutinize the bearded man. Then I spot it – the red fish tattoo on his upper left arm. I glance down at Luca laying in the bed next to me. At the red fish on his arm.

The tattoo and the arms match.

Luca rolls over in his sleep. Spoons me.

I wriggle out of his hold, and out of the bed.

On the living room table I see a pack of Luca's hand-rolled cigarettes. I haven't had a cigarette in years. I have to have one. Go out onto the porch. Light the cigarette in the dark.

A woman comes out of the house next door.

"Puedo ayudarte?"

("Can I help you?")

"Do you speak English? My Spanish is weak."

"Qué hace usted aquí?"

("What are you doing here?")

"Yo me quedo con Luca."

("I'm staying with Luca.")

"Quién es Luca?"

("Who's Luca?")

"Él vive aquí"

("He lives here.")

"Ah no señor. Ésta es la casa de la familia López. Yo estoy cuidandola mientras están en Colombia. Nó, nó, esto no es bueno. Le voy a llamar a los dueños."

("Oh, no he doesn't. This is the Lopez house. I'm watching it while they're in Colombia. No, no, this is not right. I'm going to call the owners.")

She shakes her head and angrily walks away.

I scramble to gather my clothes and pack, to just get out of there. As I'm closing up my bag, I turn and Luca is standing behind me stark naked, with a full erection and a filthy grin on his face.

He walks up to me.

Says, "Hey, good morning, early bird."

Takes my hand and moves it to between his legs.

"It's nice when you hold it," he says.

"Just hold it.

That's it."

I say, "Go back to bed. Go back to sleep. I'm going to the airport. I'll call you from New York. Go back to bed. You haven't had enough sleep."

He says, "Let's make a deal, make me come and I'll go back to bed.

Make me come. Please.

Fammi venire.

("Make me come" in Italian.)

Fammi venire

Fammi venire."

Lights shift out of that environment.

SOUND CUE NO. 3: *We hear another track from Ethan's CD entitled –*

"MISSING PERSON"

It plays beneath the scene.

It's still dark outside.

I'm struggling with my bags.

I can't find a cab.

I turn a corner and see Ethan's face on the side of a lamppost. The beautiful photo of him I took on my phone, on a missing person flyer. I'd never seen these flyers before.

I see another one on the other side of the road.

And another.

I feel like I'm hallucinating. Ethan's face on the flyers is staring at me from both sides of the street.

The faces start coming towards me.

Floating across the road.

What the hell was in that cigarette? Was it marijuana? It can't be marijuana. It must be something stronger. I never do drugs. I have no idea what it is. I tell myself just keep moving. Find a taxi. Get to the airport. You can do it. Get to the airport.

I see a brick wall covered in the flyers with Ethan's face. I feel compelled to cross the road.

I stand in front of the brick wall.

Suddenly feel the need to lay down. I go down on my knees on the sidewalk.

There's a puddle next to me. I throw water over my face from the puddle.

I have to snap out of this!

A man comes over and says, "Estás bien?"

("Are you alright?")

"Sí, gracias por detenerse. Por favor encontrarme un taxi?"

("Yes, thank you for stopping. Could you please find me a taxi?")

A taxi pulls up.

The man and the driver help me in.

And before I know it, I'm drinking espresso after espresso at the airport trying to come out of this druggy haze.

  The music ends.

The moment I get back to Brooklyn I call Stephen McCourt.

Tell him the whole thing.

As I talk on the phone I feel like I sound like a crazy person.

Stephen meets me at the café.

I show him the photo.

He says, "You can't see the man's face. It's obscured by his hair. And fish tattoos are not uncommon."

I say, "It's Luca. I recognize his body."

Stephen says, "Now so many men are going to gyms. This kind of body is everywhere."

I say, "Stephen, I know Luca intimately. That's his body."

"Does he know about Ethan?"

"Yes. He's even helped me to look for him."

"How did you meet?"

"We picked each other up in a bar. Which is not my lane. I never pick up strangers. He's been playing some kind of sick game with me!"

Stephen says I sound very distressed. I don't sound rational.

My phone rings.

"It's him! He's calling on FaceTime. What shall I do? Shall I answer it?"

Stephen says, "Yes, answer it."

I say, "Hi."

"Is this a bad time."

"I'm at work."

"I have to tell you, there's been big drama. Oh my God, the drama, Sandra. I was renting my house from a person who didn't own the house. The sweet little house you came to; it wasn't theirs to rent! They say I was trespassing. They were going to call the authorities! This leaves a terrible taste in my mouth about Puerto Vallarta. I'm going to move to Cozumel for a couple of months before I go back to school."

"So we shouldn't have been in the house?"

"No! And I paid the person I thought I was renting it from in cash, so I didn't have receipts."

"Have you been to Cozumel before?"

"No, never, but I hear there are a lot of beautiful fish off the coast. So I'll live there two months and go back to the University in Mexico City. I can see you have company. I just wanted to tell you about the big drama! I miss you. I'll talk to you when you're not busy. I love you."

And he hangs up.

Stephen says, "Well that seems to explain the angry woman next door. You have of take care of yourself, Sandra. You're vulnerable right now. You must look after yourself."

And he leaves.

> *The lights shift.*

I call Beauford.

He picks up. He's back. I re-introduce myself. Tell him I think that long-haired man he was with in Puerto Vallarta had something to do with my friend's disappearance. That I have a photo that I believe is him, can I show it to you?

Beauford says he's on his way out to go to the Museum of Modern Art. I arrange to meet him in an hour in the museum café.

> *Sandra sits. She's now with Beauford at the Museum of Modern Art.*
>
> *Beauford examines the photo on Sandra's phone.*

"Honey, I don't know if that's him. You can't see his face. I don't favor tattoos; I think I would have noticed that big ol' fish on his arm."

"Was his name Luca?"

"Oh baby, I'm sorry, I can't recall."

> *They sit in silence for a moment.*

"May I ask you something? Do you think it might be a possibility your friend Ethan found love in Puerto Vallarta, and had withdrawn himself from the world at large to luxuriate in the bliss of a romance? I ask this because when I was a young man I found love with a French boy, and no-one could reach me for months. Oh, you know what? That man I met on the beach, he had an accent that I believe was Italian. I guess I must still be quite the magnet for European men."

Lights shift.

I leave a message for Stephen. Tell him Beauford said the long haired guy had an Italian accent. I'm sure it's Luca. "With your connections can you find out if he's really attending the Universidad Anáhuac in Mexico City? His last name is M-e-s-s-i-n-a."

I'm not hearing back from Stephen, so I call the University. I hate lying but I say Luca Messina's mother has just died and I'm trying to track him down to tell him. I believe he's at your university, can you please check? The woman I'm talking to says I have to come into the administrative office. I say, "I'm calling from New York, where his mother died! I can't come in."

She puts me on hold, comes back and says, "Please don't tell anyone I gave you this information. We have no-one enrolled in our school by the name of Luca Messina. There's no-one by the name of Luca or Lucas at all."

I thank her, and hang up.

Luca is now in Cozumel.

He keeps calling. Trying to entice me into coming there. He tells me that off the island there's a sunken ship at the bottom of the sea and the sea is a color I've never imagined. And how romantic it would be.

He asks if there's any news about Ethan.

"They're still saying he was a victim of a drug deal gone bad."

"That makes no sense. He's been sober for nine years. Why would he buy drugs?"

And when I hang up, it hits me. How did Luca know Ethan was sober? And so specifically, for nine years. I've certainly never told him that. I'm going to get the truth out of him.

I fly to Cozumel.

At the Duty-free store at the airport there, I instinctively buy a couple of bottles of tequila.

Check into my hotel, and go to the little house that Luca says he's rented. It's a one story casa.

When I walk in the house, Luca seems weirdly out of it and doesn't seem happy to see me. There's something deeply unsettling about the way he's behaving.

He's on something. He's definitely on something.

I watch him as he tries to find a misplaced, clean t-shirt.

He's twitchy and agitated.

And I have this feeling of dread. I know for sure I'm right. He is the man in the photo.

He finds the t-shirt.

Says he's run out of alcohol.

I say, "I brought you some tequila."

Take the two bottles out of my bag and hand them to him.

His mood completely shifts.

He wants to take a shower.

He takes off his shirt.

My eyes zero in on that red fish tattoo.

He disappears into the bathroom.

I notice the closet door is half open.

As soon as I hear the shower water turn on I go over to it.

Luca wears his backpack everywhere. He says it's his school work. The backpack is in the closet. There are books in it and there's a thick manila envelope. I look inside. There are wads of $100 U.S. bills bound together with rubber bands. There's something solid in the side pocket. I open it. There's a hand gun in the pocket.

I look further into the closet. There's a bag of empty glass bottles with a blank sketch book and pen.

I hear the shower turn off, put everything back, return to the chair.

Luca comes out of the bathroom.

I pour him a large tumbler of tequila.

Watch him drinking.

> *We hear a pinging sound.*

I couldn't get much reception in Cozumel, so the sound of an incoming text is a surprise.

It's from Stephen McCourt.

> *Sandra reads the text aloud.*

"Ran search on Luca Messina. Sandra, please call me. Something very suspicious going on."

In spite of having taken a shower, Luca is still swirling drunk.

I refill his glass. He takes another sip.

As his eyes are focused on his drink, I reach for the phone.

Lay it down behind my bag on the table, where he won't be able to see the screen.

Press "Record" on the memo recording.

We hear a voice memo pinging sound.

"You're getting another text."

"I'm just going to ignore it, it's probably work."

I glance at the phone's screen. See the time counter moving.

My heart is in my throat.

Luca downs the tequila.

"Play that music your friend wrote."

"Ethan's music?"

"Yeah play that pretty music. You have it on your phone."

I'm thinking, the phone can't play music and record at the same time. What am I going to do?

Luca becomes louder.

"Play that pretty music! I wanna hear it!"

I remember I have my laptop in my bag. That it has Ethan's recordings on it too.

I take it out.

Say, "The sound quality on the laptop is better."

SOUND CUE NO. 4: *We hear another of Ethan's recordings from his CD –*

"UNDERNEATH"

It underscores the scene.

I pour Luca another, and glance at the phone. It's gone to the screen saver. I don't know for sure if it's still recording.

He says, "This tequila is whoah."

He moves and sits on the edge of the bed.

I say, "Oh, before I forget, David Zander says hello."

"What?"

"David Zander. David Zander asked me to say hello to you."

"What?"

"I saw him earlier today."

"What? He did not. Come on."

"I was talking to him on the beach and I mentioned you and he said you and he were friends and he asked me to say hello."

"You did not."

"I saw David Zander and he said to say hi to you."

Luca's head starts moving from side to side.

I thought he was going to pass out.

He swigs back the remaining tequila from the glass.

"David Zander is dead."

"No he's not, he says hello."

"He's dead in the sand."

"He said, 'hello.' Blond cute David Zander."

"He's not saying hello to anyone. He's under the sand. In a hole. Sandra. I buried him on Playa Bonita."

"Don't play games with me Luca, you can't have. He was with Cory Calhoun. Cory says hi too."

"What the fuck. What you fucking with me. He's in the sea. He's in the fucking sea. What are you talking about? Fuck, this is bullshit. They're both dead. I made them dead. I made them dead. You understand me? I made them dead! Don't give me this shit. I gotta lay down. This is bullshit. Bullshit!"

"How did you know Ethan had been sober for nine years?"

"'Cause he told me. Mannaggia!" *("Damn" in Italian.)*

"When?"

"On the beach when we threw the bottles."

"How did you know Ethan had been sober for nine years?"

"What's with the questions? I said, 'I got good coke.' He didn't want to be around cocaine, 'cause he was sober. I say, 'Recent sober?'

'No, nine years.'

I say, 'Come back to my room, maybe you'll want it when you see it.'

He say, 'No, no, no, I gotta go.'

And up the beach he goes.

Bye, bye, fuckin' sober people."

"Did you see him again?"

"No!

I gotta lay down. This is bullshit. Bullshit!"

He flops onto the bed, tries to get up and lunges forward and blacks out.

I touch the front of the phone. The voice memo is still recording.

Oh my God, I think, I've got him. Oh my God.

*The piano composition "UNDERNEATH"
ends.*

Grab my bag and jacket.

I'm out the front door.

I think, I was so calm. I was so calm.

I get about fifty feet and throw up on a lamppost.

I take the phone out of my pocket and play the recording. To make sure it's come out. It has. Luca's voice is recorded clearly.

Suddenly from behind, a fist punches my arm with the phone in it. It flies out of my hand. The fist belongs to a boy on a bicycle. Another boy on a bike shoves me away, scoops the phone off the sidewalk and they pedal off with it.

I scream, "Give me back the phone. Please, I will pay you for the phone! Please! I will give you money for the phone!"

They keep pedaling.

And they're gone.

I go to my hotel.

I still have Stephen's card in my purse with his cell number.

Call him from the hotel.

I tell him the whole thing.

He says, "Are you positive you're right about Playa Bonita?"

I say, "I am positive, because it made me think of the Madonna song 'La Isla Bonita.'"

Stephen makes me absolutely promise I will not go back to Luca's house. That he has to move quickly before Luca sobers up.

He contacts the police in Cozumel.

The FBI coordinate with the Mexican authorities. They raid the house and arrest Luca that night.

He denies everything, but they hold him.

They comb Playa Bonita with dogs and find David Zander's body buried under the sand.

They find Rohypnol in Luca's closet.

They re-autopsy Cory Calhoun and find a high dosage of Rohypnol, date rape drug, in his body.

Luca is extradited to the U.S.

He's in Rikers Island.

He isn't speaking at all.

The authorities tell me they don't have an airtight case without the recording. The only way they have that is if I agree to take the stand. To tell them what Luca said to me. I say, "Of course I'll do it."

He's scheduled to go on trial in New York City.

I'm all set to testify when Stephen shows up at the café.

He says, "Can we talk somewhere privately."

We go into the back office. It's a mess. Sara has gone to Canada, and I haven't replaced her. I'm depressed.

Stephen says, "Luca's real name is Luca Verro. He's the son of Calogero Verro, head of a Sicilian crime family. We feel there's a chance you may be in danger if you testify. You may start receiving threats, which could become serious. Luca is the old man's only son, and he has a reputation as being a brutal man."

"I am going to bring Luca down."

Two days later the land line in the cafe rings and a man on the other end says, "If you testify your life will end."

And then he hangs up.

I call Stephen immediately. They trace the call to a room in the Hilton Hotel in midtown Manhattan. But a room nobody is booked into.

I tell Stephen, "I will not be threatened."

A week or so goes by, I come home and on the door of my apartment someone has glued a dead, very bloody sparrow. It's completely stuck to the door. I can't get it off. The FBI come and remove it. They take the sparrow's body to see if there are fingerprints on the bird's wings.

They say, "We can move you to a hotel."

I say, "I'm not going to be frightened off."

Still every creak I hear in the apartment I jump out of my skin, or if the front door of the building slams I think, they're here!

It's ten days before the trial. The phone rings at three a.m. There's a fire at the café.

I get in a cab.

They won't let me on the block.

I say, "It's my café that's on fire!"

It takes them three hours to get the fire under control.

I go back in the morning, stand across the street. I feel like I'm having an out of body experience.

The whole café is gutted.

It looks like a smoldering charcoal cave.

Except, the wall with the chalkboard with Ethan's handwriting looks virtually untouched.

I go back to my apartment, with its single chair, and think, I have literally no-one to call.

Over the following days, many people post on the café's Facebook page. Lovely messages. But I have never felt so acutely aware of being alone.

Stephen says, "I want you to speak to a friend in the Department of Justice. If you still choose to testify I believe you qualify to be in the Witness Protection Program."

I meet with them.

They say, "We can move you to an undisclosed location."

I think, Ethan will never be able to find me.

They say, "You look concerned. Should we continue?"

She nods yes.

"We can give you a new name.

Create a different past for you.

A different back story.

Help you set up a new life.

Is this something you would like to do?"

"Yes. I want to do it. I want that new life."

"Will your husband be coming with you?"

"No, our divorce just came through."

"Children?"

"I don't have any."

"Parents? Family?"

"My birth parents are no longer living. My family disowned my mother and I after my mother married my step-father. And he's passed. So, no family. It'll just be me. Starting over. Just me."

"Very well," they say, "We'll go to your apartment and you can pack."

"Now?"

"Yes. You can take only clothing. No family photo albums. Wedding photo albums. Nothing that reveals who you once were."

They take me to my apartment. I pack clothes. Slip in Ethan's CD among them. They load my bags into a van, and drive me south.

At a certain point they say, "The location of the orientation center we're taking you to must remain unknown. We need to cover your eyes."

When they put a blindfold on me it's as though the lights go out on my old life. It's like the end of the first act of a play. The curtain coming down.

I hear the young officer sitting next to me in the van say, "Sir, the witness is weeping. The witness is weeping."

I say, "I'm not weeping, I'm just letting go. I'm just letting go."

I proceed and testify against Luca.

Luca tries to make a plea bargain by confessing to the murders, which he says were both motivated by robbery, and fueled by drugs. But it's revealed that Cory Calhoun never had any money. Which angers the judge, and doesn't help Luca at all. Still Luca maintains he didn't see Ethan after their first encounter.

He receives a forty-year prison sentence.

At the orientation center, they meet with me to establish what my new name will be.

"I want to keep the name Sandra."

I thought, I can't start responding to a different first name.

They said, "Most people do that. You can choose your new last name, or we can give you one. Obviously you can't be Sandra Jones anymore."

I said, "I'm not Sandra Jones anymore. Dwyer. It was my mother's maiden name. I'll be Sandra Dwyer."

They said, "You can't have any name a relative has, or has had."

"Then, Rivers. My step-father was a musician. He loved the saxophone player Sam Rivers."

They asked, "Do you want to think about it?"

"I have thought about it. I'll be Sandra Rivers."

"And you can request the kind of area where you would like to be re-located."

"On a coast. In reach of a city or major town, if that's possible."

And I could tell they liked me, the way they responded, "We can't guarantee anything."

"But we'll see what we can do."

After a few days, they tell me they've established where my re-location will be. Northern California. A coastal town called Jenner.

They've found a small house there. They'll give me money to live on for up to six months or till I find a job. They give me the name of an inspector. A point of contact person in California. They give me a driver's license with my new name. A credit card. A phone.

They say, "Here is your plane ticket to San Francisco leaving tomorrow. When you get to San Francisco the inspector will meet you at the airport with a government car you can keep for up to six months."

"That's it. Then I'm on my own?"

"Basically."

When I come out of baggage claim a man is holding a sign that reads, "Rivers." It takes me a second to realize, oh that's me.

He says, "Walk out with me as though I'm the car service you booked. The house you'll be living in is empty. There's no furniture. Nothing. It's tiny, but quite near the sea. Here are the keys. There's a map in the front seat of the car with the address. We had a shortage of vehicles. It's an older model, but it's in good condition."

We load my bags.

I sit in the driver's seat.

He says, "Call when you need us to make up job references under your new name. Good luck to you."

And walks away.

I sit there in the front seat of the car, thinking, this is a very old car.

It has a CD player.

I think, put on Ethan's music. There's that beautiful last track on the CD titled, "Destination."

> **SOUND CUE NO. 5:** *We hear –*

> "DESTINATION"

> *It underscores the following.*

And I drive.

Pull off at a strip mall to a bedding store. Buy a folding bed, sheets and a pillow, load it in the back of the car, notice a liquor store, think, get a bottle of wine, it'll relax your nerves, then think, no, you don't need that, get in the car and continue.

Up the coast.

Thinking, I have absolutely no idea where I'm headed.

I am absolutely driving into the unknown.

I start looking for work. Thinking I want to try to find some kind of job connected to music. There's nothing in the area. No jobs that sound interesting at all. I go down to Bodega Bay, all along the coast. I find a quite beautiful restaurant on the side of a cliff overlooking the sea. There's a large empty room at the back of the place. Once rented out for private events. Now no longer in use. I say to the owner, "This could be a music room. For jazz, singer-songwriters, cabaret. Not strictly one kind of music. Expand the restaurant into here. You could have music."

The owner says, "If you do all the work to set it up, I'll try your music idea."

It works.

After a year, the room has fully become a venue for music, and I curate and book the music.

I have a sexy fling with a sweet park ranger called Teddy. And feel relief that when everyone is asked at a New Year's Eve party I go to, "Who have you had the sexiest time with in your life thus far?"

I can now answer park ranger Teddy and not Luca.

Though at that same party they ask, "Who have you felt the purest love for?"

I slip out to the bathroom. And in the bathroom I think of what Ethan had said the last night I spent with him.

That he felt like disappearing from his life, but that we were so simpatico that if he vanished, I'd probably disappear from my life too.

"DESTINATION" *ends.*

When I get home I sit by my computer.

My email address is new.

I remember Ethan's.

I type it into the recipient address.

Write – "This is Sandra. Are you there?"

Sit in the dark of my living room.

Glance at the screen.

There's a reply.

"Yes. Yes, I'm here."

I step outside my house.

Stand in the night air.

And think, I knew it. I knew you were still alive. That's all I need to know. And that you're still out there.

And in the dark I walk down to the beach.

Across the sand.

To the shoreline.

Stand looking out at the ocean.

And I suddenly remember something I'd completely forgotten.

When I was a child, the teacher at my school went around the class asking all the children, "What do you think you're going to do when you grow up?"

One by one each child replied.

"I want to be a ballerina when I grow up."

"I want to be a vet."

"I want to be soccer player."

And when the teacher came to me she asked, "And what do you think that you're going to do when you grow up, Sandra?"

I answered, "Live by the ocean in California, so whenever I like, I can look out at the sea. I can listen to music and look out at the sea."

"That doesn't sound like a life," she said. "That sounds like a dream."

> *We hear the lapping of waves on a shore.*

> **SOUND CUE NO. 6:** *With the shimmering sounds of Ethan playing his recorded composition –* "LIKE A DREAM (ENDING)"

> *Sandra looks out over the water.*

> *The lights close in on her, and slowly fade.*

The End

> *The lights come up for bows and the bow music –*

> **SOUND CUE NO. 7:** "WHO I HAVE LOVED THE MOST (BOWS)"

> *The composition continues as the audience exits the theatre. Even if all the audience has left, it still plays to the end.*

MUSIC CUE NOTES

SANDRA is scored like a film, as Sandra sometimes musically scores scenes in her life as if they are happening in a movie. In the original production the timings of where the words in the script lined up with the music was precise. Largely determined by the composer, Matthew Dean Marsh. Here is a list of them, as an approximate guide that doesn't wish to completely lock the actor in, or inhibit an original performance, but give a road map. They're all quite logical. Intended as a guide.

1. "Love Theme from an Imaginary Movie Entitled Sandra"

Cue 0:00 "And in my head I'm thinking, my marriage really is over."

00:13 "What is this music?"

00:43 "I spoke to Ethan almost every day."

01:28 "I keep thinking I'll find clues"

02:14 "imaginary to me... Come here."

02:25 "The following morning, while Luca's still sleeping"

2. "Further and Further"

Cue 0:00 "headphones..."

00:03 "...and walk a little way into the sea."

00:10 "Then further."

00:14 "And further."

00:22 "I wish I could swim with the music playing in my ears."

00:32 "I wish I could go far out to sea with"

00:39 "I imagine drowning"

01:00 "Who will be the last person I speak to in my life?"

01:22 "A child swimming under the water"

Music cuts out right after "off the headphones."

3. "Missing Person"

Cue 0:00 after "Fammi venire."

00:02 "It's still dark outside."

00:11 "and see Ethan's face"

00:25 "I see another one"

00:29 "And another."

00:36 "The faces start coming towards me."

00:56 "I see a brick wall"

01:10 "I go down on my knees"

01:20 "I have to snap out of this!"

01:34 "A taxi pulls up."

01:46 "druggy haze."

4. "Underneath"

Cue 0:00 after "laptop is better."

00:10 "This tequila is woahhh."

00:20 "Oh, before I forget, David Zander says hello."

00:55 "David Zander is dead."

01:15 "Don't play games with me Luca,"

01:32 "I made them dead. You understand me?"

01:47 "This is bullshit. Bullshit!"

02:18 "Bye, bye, fuckin' sober people."

02:34 "He flops onto the bed,"

02:43 "I've got him."

5. "Destination"

Cue 0:00 after "titled, 'Destination.'"

00:02 "And I drive."

00:25 "Up the coast."

00:29 "I have absolutely no idea where I'm headed."

00:57 "There's a large empty room"

01:04 "This could be a music room."

01:20 "It works."

01:30 "I have a sexy fling"

01:48 "I can now answer park ranger Teddy and not Luca."

02:02 "I slip out to the bathroom."

6. "Like A Dream (Ending)"

Cue after the final line. Last chord hits on blackout.

7. "Who I Have Loved the Most (Bows)"

Played during the bows, and as the audience exits. The track should play all the way to the end, even if there's no-one remaining in the theatre.